the men at my white table

a Collection

by Matilde Tomat Dall'Oglio

Copyright ©2017 Matilde Tomat

All Rights Reserved.

All words and photographs by Matilde Tomat, unless quoted otherwise.

No part of this publication may be reproduced, distributed, or transmitted in any form or by any means, including photocopying, recording, or other electronic or mechanical methods, without the prior written permission of the author / publisher, except in the case of brief quotations embodied in critical reviews and certain other non-commercial uses permitted by copyright law.

For permission requests, please contact the Author.

The Author is available for presentations, workshops and talks.

Tomat, Matilde.
The Men at My White Table: a Collection / Matilde Tomat

1. Fiction 2. Short Stories

APR 2017 - First Edition
MAY 2018 – First paperback version

This is for you.

> "Simple confession isn't that powerful, Josef.
> If it were, there'd be no neurotic Catholics!"
> [Irvin D Yalom, When Nietzsche Wept]

acknowledgements

There are people without whom this book would never have been possible: Margherita Gliubich who was there and still is; Roberto Maniacco: I really hope there's plenty of fishing wherever you are.

David Kemp who taught me to stay with silence; Fran Cullen who helped me recognise my intellectual loop; Deborah Smith for marking a very embarrassing first draft; Samantha Crapnell, Kerry Gormley and Helen Boswell for being part of my tribe; Ian Scott for the Checkov&Cheese Collective; David Samuel Randall for his editorial support.

Nicoletta Bello for being Nicoletta Bello.

Giovanni Villa for shapeshifting into my personal St. Christopher and Simone A De Cia for using that whiteboard in my living-room.

And all the men at my white table.

*****

Matilde Tomat Dall'Oglio is an attentive and meticulous traveller, able to walk without stumbling along wearisome and faraway paths, able to investigate the substance of her research and dissolve it in the clearness of the psychological investigation. (...) This work of Matilde Tomat Dall'Oglio is found at the centre of a creative journey which isn't at all finished. Hers is a work more rooted in a personal suffering than a programmatic manifesto, fuller of anger and anxiety, more elemental and passionate. The style also follows an original and dry pace, discerning and sophisticated, but at the same time simple and essential, and which distinguishes the whole work.
(Marzia Bergo, from her preface to *Beyond the Ninth Wave*,1999)

*****

Images and words together create a conversation, give a rhythm, suggest an atmosphere. Even in the writing we find the rhythm and resonances which proceed from a choice to "play with the words", to distil the meaning, penetrating deeper in the meander of the language in order to look for new expressions via the audacious combination which could render "speakable" what is felt in the deepest darkness of inwardness. The effort to say what you can barely recognise as an inner overwhelming urgency is a challenge that poetry has taken on itself for a while. "I breathe the nostalgia / really of those cain lips / on my athenaic bosoms / when no more impregnable / I was free to love", says Matilde, calling together the nostalgia of a past experience and a vertigo stud in memory. This is the power of the word: the coming back of a repressed emotion even if never really forgotten and lost in the many forms of reality-in-becoming. (...) Matilde Tomat has a fairly long experience which connects her to photography; (...) it seems that the model that she follows is the one of the cognitive scrutiny in the broadest sense, as if the instrument was another eye, able to read the world beyond human senses, or better, beyond the foreseeable rationality of our customary seeing. As if through the camera (but we know it is an automatic action) we could find something that the unconscious already perceives but that our eyes cannot yet see. Something disturbing if known but at the same time foreigner, wrongfooted, scary. The choice to capture a shadow, to fill an absence. *(Gabriella Musetti presenting the art installation *Words&Photos*, Cividale del F. July 2008)*

about the author

Matilde Tomat Dall'Oglio is a writer, photographer, counsellor, and story-teller.

While concentrating on details and minutiae and being seduced by black&white, s/loves choosing themes and subjects where her imagination (or neat casualness) allows her to break conceivable rules and to play with the magic of shapes.

She is a strong believer in her desire to represent simplicity and devoidness, regardless of the medium used. Inspired by that ephemeral boundary between personal and universal pain, she is interested in eternity as a long progression of here&now's. She doesn't do "lifetime".

She published two books and exhibited her photographic works on numerous occasions.

Described as congruent and very human, her art (work/life/being) is founded on unearthing the root while discarding the superfluous.

Born in Italy, she now lives in UK.

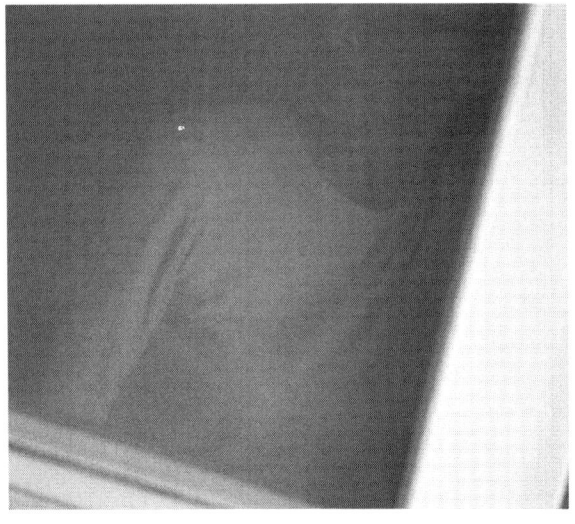

contents

acknowledgements 4
about the author 7
in memory of a man 13
M is my name 17
beyond the ninth wave 21
ludus 27
the end of the meal 35
never my lips 43
half a tear 47
don't touch me 55
lk 59
the elegance of the equation 63
remission 73
as tempest 77
something cool 81
in that dream 89
drafted in pain 93
find/ness me 99

1: feels like home

in memory of a man

in memory of a man

lost

not forgotten

bunch roses 5

of indefinite hue

'with immense love'

thought and never written

(1996)
to my father

2: *mazzo rose 5*

M is my name

miht-hilð ~ mori-gena ~ mor-rigan ~ myrddhin ~ modron ~ mat

and while the roots sink

in the outline of the mountains up north

I find pastures and vineyards

in pearly grey photographs

and ungainly poses,

because the soul cannot be engraved

and I recognize hands and glances

gestures millenniums old

I recognize names and verses

sing-songs and garlands

diffident that Woman who wore

my same name with respect

thing of old times

they haven't let her die

M is my name.

3: territories

beyond the ninth wave
– extract from p.24 of the original edition in Italian

I wrote *Oltre la Nona Onda* (Beyond the Ninth Wave) back in Italy in 1996 after "Beowulf, a plausible hypothesis"; I was sitting at a small desk in a corner of the living room, next to a window, and was protected by a faithful pair of raven, perched on a dead pear tree. Once I finished the story, they left and I never saw them again.

This short book was published in 1999 by Oppure, won two prizes, toured libraries and cultural circles; and it was turned into a theatre production for one night only, to be performed by faithful friends under an oak tree.

My ex-husband said at the time that this book was the first thing he saw me beginning and ending. Our marriage was another one.

I have been offered twice to have it main-stream published, with some minor tweaks, but I have always said no. Morrigan, my main character, is part of me; or better: she is me. She is family. It's a book I always go back to regardless of the groping and affected style I can now recognise.

Morrigan and I decided to trust you and here is an extract, slightly amended, of her story.

***

I see the valley underneath, and the waves; I can perceive the undertow reaching for me in between the leaves, which whispers a lament of the forgotten days: a story of a man and a woman in love who have been separated, and who cannot be together anymore. Destiny has been cruel with them. They cannot laugh. They will not touch each other's hands anymore. Their lips will not kiss, neither with initial modesty, nor with passion. I turn and run away, among the foliage that once befriended me but now bear resemblance to arms which want to grab me and hold me.

Once, in this wood, you kissed me; and I, happy, danced between the branches and I let myself be caressed and pleased by the leaves but now they scrape my legs while I run fast, the hem lifted so not to stumble; they scratch my face, Wulf, that face you have caressed, and I can't understand anymore if it's dewdrops or tears rolling down my cheeks, mixed with the warmth of the blood. My dress, the one I thought about wearing for your comeback, is torn and its colour is not brilliant anymore. May I be damned for wearing it that day, the day you had me sent here. Why did you want this?

I go back now to that place you have decided to send me, in that cave, under the oak tree. It's an old cavity, and it's bare. My Lord, you could have chosen another place to let me await the end of my days in solitude, not under an oak tree. I am not like it. I look at it, its leaves, fruits; branches.

Wulf, what did you want to do with our affection? I was just happy when I heard you saying that you would never betray me. I now understand: you betray someone you love, and you never loved me. From there, there where you are, beyond those waves, in a foreign land, you have asked your Mother to take me here. And obviously, she was content to oblige and with her proud and arrogant insolence she materialised my Ninth Wave; she has made it real, tangible, eternal. "Your Lord has asked me to find for you another arrangement. I'm now asking you to follow whoever I will send for you tomorrow. As of now, please leave us and retire to your chamber."

Wulf, I am not like this oak, strong and sturdy. I am weak, lonely. I am a woman, alone among this chatty crowd who is never silent and reminds me of your kisses, of your hands. Wulf, I asked only to be close to you; I thought you wanted the same. You deceived me. I deceived myself. Now I reconsider everything that has been said and where there was warmth, now it is only darkness, pain and crying. You have discovered with me the seasons of my body, my emerging, and we laughed together about it; you even gently teased me. And now, this body I thought you liked, won't be needed anymore. I feel I have lost something and I cannot understand what it is that I am missing: is something tangible or only mental? Can it be only a thought?

But you can't heal from your thoughts. Do you remember the young Freawaru, after the death of her husband? The Abbot said that her grief would have weakened in time. Her thinking was ill and she did not heal. She was wondering in those miserable dark rooms while talking to herself, but as soon as you spoke to her, she fell silent and stared at you with empty eyes; it appeared she was asking if there had been any rumours about her partner, her accomplice, if you knew when he would come back. Do you remember, My Lord, of her hair? It turned into spotless tow when she heard of his death; it was all one with her pale face and the paraments of the Abbot: a mask. And as much as we tried to liven her up, she simply crumpled. Do you remember, My Lord, her hands? They became thin and gnarled, dry twigs, not young anymore, and eager to hold life with joy, but they constantly intertwined with each other, never ceasing. She did not heal from her thinking. If she lost her house, or food, she wouldn't have become that. But when you lose your thoughts, Sir, your, our life has no sense. Have you seen her lately? Have you ever really looked at her? Go back there, and look at her, on top of the hill, that gonfalon of sadness, rags and twigs silently screaming; listen to that cry coming out from that blood; think about the clanging of that thought, all the pain that has happen to her.

I do not want to become like that.

ludus

garden of shadows in waxing moon

and of waning feelers

of downtimes

souls are lingering

in a malvaceous must.

lean out to seize

deprive to protract

glances of thousand eyes

patrolling

(1997)
to ludus

4: My name is Jenny

I breathe the nostalgia

I breathe the nostalgia
really of those cain lips
on my athenaic bosoms
when no more impregnable
I was free to love.

and now, in this foreign orchard
among white wither tulips
contemplate on this last drop
sliding down my womb
exposed, after the storm.

with my thinking I push it lower
Feminine herself in her trembling and hesitating.
the voice of that man so adult and deep
that celebrated my name
again and again and again
now for other bosoms, for other loins.

my cold feet
white in this moonless night
facing south, there force me to stop.

that last icy drop
yet falling turning east
as if to call him. she then stops
to await her sister, brackish,
not collected by my lips.

and I see the profile of that man
reflexed in the two sisters
no more separated, but smelted
the saltiness of one lost in the other.

appears smiling, as in times of yore.
again, and again and again
while the omphalos howled his name

(040508)

5: *rummer soldiers*

the end of the meal

And then you are sitting there, around a table. The food is warm in front of you, and the glasses are full, and you have been given the best place to sit, surrounded by smiling friends who pat your hand while you eat. You talk about books, and music and places discovered, and others to visit again.

One bite, slowly. And then another one, very slowly; your eyes closed, smiling. And then another, slightly faster.

You have helped to prepare the table and the offering is way more than a simple dish of something. The proffering is a lesson, of which you know nothing about.

Because then someone makes a comment while serving the pie. I never liked sentences which begin with: "you know what: you…"; but she is right. "I have really got to tell you, that you…". Her husband is bowing his head in silence while she slowly but steadily morphs words into images, fitting the scenario with precision.

The more I listen, the more I don't like what I hear, and I would just like to leave. I wonder where I put the keys to my car and think of any

excuse to just silently flush myself out of the chair, flow past the kitchen, past the hall and not stop until I break and crumble at the front door; but, instead, the more I sit there, the more I nod.
That last bite is still being chewed and doesn't want to be swallowed. And I feel thrown back years in another country and in another kitchen, with curly blond hair and someone else patting my hand, while I cry in a soup.

And then forward again: another city, another kitchen, a closer past: I break a glass, I cut my hand and the only thing that I can utter is: "I should have really gone home this morning". I'm told "don't be silly" but that morning, when I woke up and turned on my left and looked at his back and caught a glimpse of his tattooed shoulder, long grey hair and a gentle humming in his sleep, so beautiful and so warm, I just wanted to go home.
The selfish me.
I have to admit, aloud, what I always knew.

So, tonight, over some dry tomatoés, I finally name all the things I will really miss, which can be counted on my three ringed fingers. And I realize what I wanted and never asked for.

Because, you see, when you cook you know when something is missing. So, you expectantly open that cupboard to the right, the one just above the microwave, and you rummage through little colourful bottles, and you frantically open them and sniff them and then your nose dives into the right one because they found each other: buds, skin and spice. They called each other, and you have only been a spectator of this summoning so now you can smile because your guts, through your nose, know that that One is the ingredient which was missing. Because it takes you back in time, and then forward into the future, and away to some distant shores; it takes you back home and to unvisited lands. And I don't know how but you find yourself eager and ready to choose to learn new recipes every day.

But instead you open, sniff, and close; and put away one, two, more bottles and each and every one make that distinctive disappointed sound once back in the cupboard: a symphony to the worthlessness of the spice. Then you sit and eat in a silence broken only by yawns and fake smiles until you openly acknowledge that "there is still something missing": that concealed, elusive, mysterious ingredient you cannot name.

You cannot fool the chefs.

And when I said: "you deserve the best that I can be", it turned out the worst that I am. Because it's not me. Because I tiptoed throwing a toothbrush in a bag instead of dancing bare feet with my long uncombed hair until I felt I could simply head home.

So, I have added flavours and ingredients covering up honest food, creating a cacophony of overshadowing tastes fighting for supremacy, never following the book. I made my own book.

And all this because I was cooking at the right of the most generous chef you could ever find; the one who told me I was never in the way; and I thought it would have been sinful that the ungrateful me, given the opportunity, would have simply gone home. Because he sharpened the knives, he gave me the apron and offered his kitchen.

"What about if someone simmers and the other one boils", I asked once. But I knew even then that the unspoken question I wanted an answer for was: "what about if I simmer and you, the chef, boil?" and so I thought I was a bad bad girl, that I wasn't putting enough effort in learning new recipes. If he was boiling, I should have boiled too. And like a sour medieval concoction stolen from a pagan book, I blamed out loud the wind, my female mood and a cursed spell. When unseen, I danced more, unruled hair and bare feet; and stopped eating when alone.

But my forte, you see, are colourful and happy salads, and strawberries with vinegar, and spritz with aperol. I like the saltiness of caperberries when they break under your teeth with that distinctive sound and their juice floods your mouth; I make love feeding the other one a grape stolen while cycling in the sun, I tango on spilled flour on the kitchen floor. I improvise words for new menus. My senses are alert to fresh linen cloths which prepare my buds for the food to come; I can laugh out loud out of pure ecstasy when the fig is finally open revealing its sacred inner self. Now I know: I can only do what I am good at. I am a good chef, but I was in the wrong kitchen. Following a recipe is not me. And I tried too hard to fit among the ingredients. And the chef, who was so ecstatic to have found me in a foreign market, among red beef heart tomatoes and the bitterness of rocket and crisp white wine, and cherished his treasure, brought me home only to find that there are no recipes in all his books for which he could use me day after day after day.

At the first dinners the mouthfuls were frantic and eager, and turned into juicy hungry bites. And we talked and made love and laughed and talked and made love and laughed. By the distinctive way he called my name, I knew I existed. And then we confessed and discovered and laughed; and in the end cooked together. So we stopped talking. "We should have probably also danced. We would have been great", I thought before that long taste of bitter chocolate, forgetting he had no sense of rhythm. And at the gargantuan evening feast, among laughter and wine and crispy prawns and tender crabs, we appeared happy. The air was tangible and the scent of food then melted into my intense innermost sacred mood and his earthy hands celebrated and secured his harvest.

Not long after I started wilting. The pot was too small for the water I needed. But the chef was so gentle and keen and helpful and such a maestro that I sucked from that little pot all the resources I had and knew, and still showed my shiny leaves in the sun. From the top I was moved to the window sill, while in the kitchen he was still looking for a recipe. Because he tried, oh he tried. Then I was moved outside, on the bench. The clouds came and the rain followed; the water was too much for my little pot and I felt like drowning. The herb lost its fragrance and the chef sat staring at his hands. He then stood up, emitted his resigned sigh and finally admitted that there is no recipe, not that he couldn't find one.

That morning, I should have really gone home.

So tonight, while driving home with the taste of sun-blushed dried tomatoes still in my mouth, fused with the saltiness of anchovies and tears on my lips, I smile at that couple that I see avidly tasting each other, lit briefly while I turn left.

"I think that me and you will take different roads, and it's sad" he said over the phone. There and then I concocted for him, in a cauldron, sadness, surprise and hurt, added just a pinch of apple and bitter orange leaves, and crushed periwinkles while, all of a sudden, I felt distinctively hungry.

And here, now, at my white table, in this strangely silent night, among sweet watery strawberries, slices of juicy oranges, the un-revealed bitterness of a deep red liquor and the crispness of some north-eastern bubbling wine, my body resounds at the lost potentiality. Head tilted back, I wail for that accomplice at my left, that conspirator in fusing different tastes and textures, that person who listened and talked, and confessed, and discovered, and laughed; who danced with me on spilled flour, his hand on my neck; that One I haven't yet met.

If only I could simply go home just after the strawberries.

never my lips

never my lips
were allowed
to rest
there.

tortured.

but at night
impulsive
and not seen
they trace back
convulsed
that stretch
satisfied.

as if
they made it already
theirs.

and you, to them

had

granted permission.

grateful now.

(120702)
to S.: does he remember?

6: *lovers entwined*

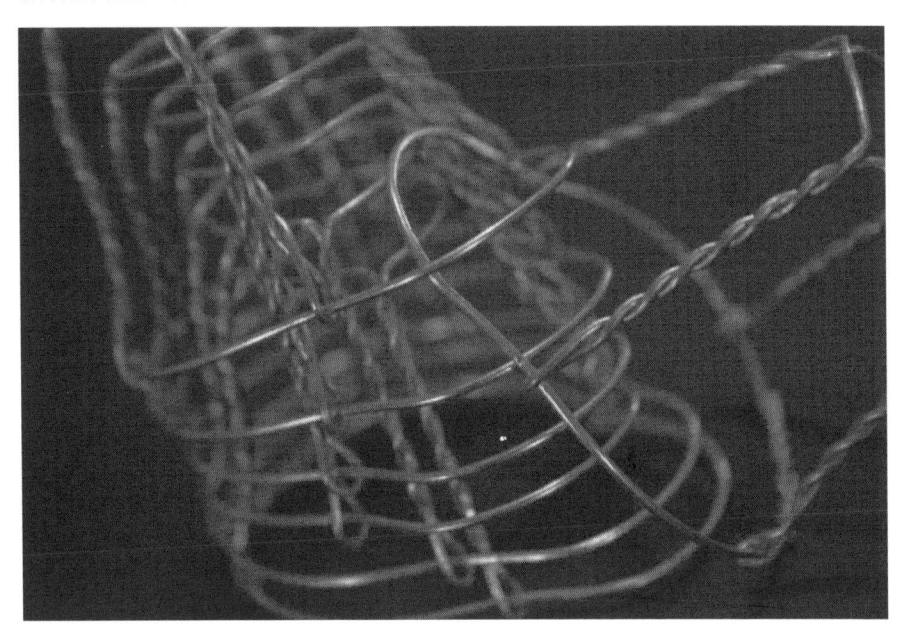

half a tear

>   Wherever I'll choose to go, whomever
>   I will love in future,
>   Nothing and no one ever
>
>   I will allow no one to take away those few things of yours I'm left with:
>
>   A foulard
>   3 inked sheets
>   Half a tear (no one ever saw the other half),
>   A sharp glance,
>   10 drops of water (so spoiled),
>   The trace of a hand
>
>   You survive with what you are given.
>   [Udine 1996 – for P. – vorrei essere l'aria che sostiene il tuo volo]

She sat there in front of me, with a sense of urgency, and it felt as if she was still floating, gently swaying from side to side on my red sofa while adjusting her skirt. Acute, sharp, precisely eloquent, perfectly dressed.

>   [I acknowledge one single shallow breath in my own chest,
>   A skip in the flow: where is that coming from?]

The story unfolds and she tells me of this pain. She describes it at times numb and at times sharp; "It has a life on its own, you see; it's within me, I am breeding this pain".

…

"How painful is this pain?"

"I don't know.

[hitting her erroneous Moho continuity.]

But it's always there and if I try to hold it, it vanishes. And then it appears again, with the sound of broken laughter and a scorning honk".

Her focal point, wherever she was looking, vanishes instantly from her eyes, leaving behind lifeless cheeks and pale lips. I am ready to see her transfigure into tiny pieces of white paper tossed at the wind; and then: disappear.

Her voice turns into a plea, and this hour into a homily about rejection. Amen.

[Misery.]

"I can't let myself go, I need to hold this, whatever this is, all together. That honk, that laughter is painful and it's gently and mercilessly executing me. I can't afford to be seen like this.

[I confess to almighty God,

and to you, my brothers and sisters,

that I have loved.]

I don't even know why I am here and what I am looking for but this pain is unbearable and this vanishing and then reappearing at the most inappropriate moments is too much please help me and tell me what to do please tell me I am not going mad this sound this sound scornful all these voices in my head and one tells me to stop and the other one suggests that I need to be punished and all this doesn't make sense

(She finally breaths).

She stops to look at her hands and the right one is slightly shaking. She adjusts the skirt again and massages her right thigh.

[Her pose is of porcelain and reminds me of my grandmother when sitting in the communal lounge waiting for us to come and visit on an, otherwise, unplanned and boring Sunday afternoon.]

I know that people would think I am mad and that I don't know the value and significance and meaning of love. I mean, I think I have always loved him. Since I first met him. I saw him and I can feel now exactly the same sensations: my heart slowed down, I gasped for air, I felt slightly dizzy. I think I died a little bit. Yes, absurd, I know. But I can assure you that on that Monday morning I actually died. I was there and he was there. I mean, it must have been a Monday, at work, back there and back then. He simply smiled and that was it. Nothing more. Just a smile. Oh, no, it wasn't even a smile. He probably was more smirking than anything else, looking at me; me, the apprentice. And, you know, I was more the apprentice than he could ever have realised. I turned, he was there, well, his hand was there. I saw his left hand first: do you know that space where the abductor separates from its tendon, and the artery signals danger; that empty pool of salty water for my heart so thirsty and my lips suddenly dry? That's what I saw.

And then I raised my eyes and I saw him and I couldn't understand anything anymore. I felt small, young, refreshed, embarrassed; alive and yet dead. Unreachable. Un-reachable. That's what he is. And was.

I mean, nothing has changed since. That honking sound that pulsates in my cells is a constant reminder that he is inaccessible, unapproachable; and that I am now old, boring, and living with a cat. I am boring and he is unreachable. Do you mind if I stand up? I need to stand up.

(She now paces gently up and down the room, that sound of expensive shoes on the floor when shushed by rubber.)

Do you understand me? Do I make any sense? Will this ever end? And if it ends, what will I be left with? If I don't have this, what will it be of me? I am trying, really, to act on my best behaviour. I can't afford to be seen like this, it's like I'm rotting from the inside. But the other day, I left home with the door wide open, you see… I can't allow it. I just can't. I left for work, the sun was shining like on that Monday, the air was smelling of warmth, and I really thought he was there, next to me, in this city, in my car. I could swear I saw him, and then I thought: you stupid woman… and then, what if he is dead and he really is here… and then again: you stupid stupid idiot! So, I went, I went to work for the whole day with my front door wide open.

(She stops to take a slow breath and looks around.)

I can't love. I don't want to love. I do not want to be loved. A colleague, well no, a friend, he is a friend. You see, he came close to me, the other evening, and he hugged me and looked at me straight in my eyes, and he played with my nose, with his nose, oh my God it was cheap and embarrassing and childish, I don't even know why I am telling you this anyway, it was embarrassing and scary and he didn't let go. It was dark, we were outside. You see, this is my space, my body, my skin. Yes, it was like if my coat and jacket and shirt and skin had been peeled away, and he was touching my flesh and hugging me and I could feel his breath, I mean, the warmth of his breath, the cigarettes he smoked, and I thought that I did not want to smell him so I stopped breathing and then I closed my eyes, tight, as I did when I was a kid and I told him, half laughing: oh, please, don't kiss me, please don't kiss me, but inside I was dying again. I do not want to be touched.

[Annie, oh sister Annie...]

Sorry if I'm pacing like this but it's my back no it's not my back oh I feel like all itchy as if I were about to shed my skin and why can't I just be normal, eh? Why can't I? Fucking hell, oh sorry for swearing, I just can't allow to be seen like this and if I change, if I if I allow this vulnerable side of me to come to the surface all that I have worked for will vanish. All the love I felt, and feel for him, will vanish."
"All the love will vanish..."
"Yes, if I stop hurting, it's like the love is not real and has never been real and I have wasted 17 years of my life. Me, useless as a Virgin in Paradise".

She stops, smiles at me, and composedly sits on the sofa again, gasping.

[Seventeen years, I think. We stay in silence, for a while. I pretend I let her be but, you know, the truth is that there is a plant, on a windowsill,

next to the picture of a man.

That plant is a dying plant.

That plant is kept on the verge of death on purpose,

that plant is made to suffer.

As long as that plant is neither dead nor alive,

there's breath in that instance in between. Pain-by-proxy.

Ténle vive l'anime in me... I can hear myself humming.

I silently uncross (voluptuously?) and then cross my legs again, turn

slightly to my left, towards the sun filtering through two large

windows and I try to remember

how long it has been since the last time I watered it

and if my client has noticed

the two tiny dry leaves still hanging in there.

A comforting painful justice. Smirking, now.

Me and you, stupid plant, we are not quite done yet.]

don't touch me

don't touch me

while my glance flees yours
(shivers, I look beyond your shoulder)
don't look for my severe eyes
(heroic)
a veil of shells
and laces of thin seaweeds
acts as my armour
(now)
merciful
(dontouchmescaremeyousay)
wait, you mumble
what, I ask
(lips)
(don't hold out your arms at me)
don't even stroke me
(my skin rough sand)
and don't stop while
(ruthless)
and don't look for me when
(rejected)
I leave with a luggage
full of bats
(rains now, sarcastic)
on a cloud of vapour and saltiness
(inexorable)
my skin of coffee
(ungrateful)
for other hands
for other glances
(fierce)
while tears weave necklaces
of pearls to be undersold in the street

(another kiss?)
(bland)
hence I look and thoughts ideas designs outlines
torments opinions inspirations old movies slide away
what a shame, a shabby love

(280501)

7: loneliness

Ik

will let you catch a glimpse of me
from those windows with no sail

will impinge
slow as sweet sap.

I have infused and conquered
taken by storm

I will let you haul
from that harbour with no wings

and the tears, now
will only be yours
for my straight back

as Mother
proud and raging
while at steady steps
I cover the music
of my going

(200608)

8: a glimpse

the elegance of the equation

"I am a writer", I state, balancing olives on a paper plate. There is no brown bread and too many voices.

"Have you published anything?", he asks.

"Oh, no. Not an author. I just write. A writer. I write 1000, at times 2000 words a day. It's not that I write something. I just write. Of course, I do write words, but I am more interested in how the letters are linked together, the pitch and fall of the stroke."

The balance between void and full, the distance between words, their privacy: do they feel (the words, I mean) their boundaries pushed? You do not need words. Not to create anything of any literary or artistic value. Just the passing of time, my personal Japanese garden, a mono-surface ikebana. I am more absorbed by the noise of the nib, a tenuous scratching at ivory paper. Scratching and revealing by adding ink and subtracting fibres. I substitute what's already there with something new. I am ploughing and seeding. I replace emptiness and at the same time expose one of the infinite possible combination of signs and marks, all-present but hidden in a page. What's the nib doing in me? Sometimes I wonder if the line I'm creating is three dimensional, or not. Could we magnify it, its own breadth would appear. So, I fancy that it would. The queue hasn't moved passed the pork pies for a while now.

"At times, I ponder on the hovering dot (I mime something somewhere, suspended half way in the air, by nothing) that one that is not right in the middle of the space, but just below the midpoint. A point at midpoint. His higher outer skin teasing the imaginary half-way mark of the empty space, dancing between two lines (did I just say "his"?). Somehow, I think that writing, in this way, controls and therefore codifies Beauty. I'm in the act of making my own world a better place. It gives a sense of order, balance. It makes things simpler. There's no Χάος on my pages."

(I am wondering if there is any bread, brown bread. I cannot eat olives and pâté without brown bread.) Filling that space, to me, is never pointless. It is a quest for the perfect conjunction between an ideal pen, faultless paper, the moment; and me. I am mesmerized by the ease of the sign, the sliding of the pen, the weight of my wrist, the length of my nails on the barrel; the impeccable blend of voluptuousness and angst. A sensuous ritual.

It's not writing, it's not drawing. It's flowing. It's continuity.

"What do you think makes the perfect writing?", I ask.

"A good plot?", he replies.

"Is it just the words, or the sense, the feelings someone is trying to transmit? I am wondering if a person reading my writing, would feel the exact same emotions as I feel when I write."

Impossible, and frustrating. Sometimes I question if it is more my experience that's important: me as I write. Actually, me as I am writing. I am writing. Writing. Write-ing. In the moment. (He places some white bread on my plate. I don't want white bread.) There is a beginning and there is an end, and both happen now. "When I am sitting at my white table, in front of the window and I hold my pen, I breathe New York at Christmas, I hear Woody Allen, I wear the elegance of a velvety black dress, I'm in a yellow cab. *Aht to leh-vadh.*"

"Oh, you've been to New York?"

"No, I have never been there."

My glasses slide down, slowly; he pushes them up gently with his little finger, juggling plates, plastic forks and napkins. Boundaries pushed. Which words are we? The process of me writing is fuelled and filled by what I smell, what I see, how I feel, any odd sensations I'm brewing within in my body. (My dish feels heavier. Breadsticks? Sticks as cyphers. What do they remind me of?) Do I need to transfer this onto paper? Of course, not. Are my words as long as my thoughts; or my writing as fast as my thinking? Time slows down and I can breathe. Am I recording also the sentence in between? (He glares through me, head slightly tilted. Can he see the discourse silently falling from my head? As a concert of thuds-on-mute of disarticulated Lego pieces falling to the floor. For a second, I look at my shoes.)

"If I write one word, would it evoke the same imagery in someone else's mind?"

"Whatchyamean?"

"If I say, or write the word Tree, I do have an image. Is the same image for everybody? I see chestnuts and maybe others see pines. If I write chestnuts, would we imagine the same solitary tree, on the same hill, in the sun? I find this fascinating, because no matter how hard we try to communicate, our minds will keep on seeing the world as we have always seen it, through our eyes only. That's our reference, our own code: us. You see, there is no such a thing as true communication. I spent one summer studying Akkadian, you know (𒀭 𒀸 𒀹 𒀼 I try to mime), logograms, just for fun. Archaic symbols. No communication."

Me on a quest, looking for hidden meanings. Semi-optic. Breadsticks! Now instead a present-ologists of papery symbolism, something private, something mine only. Pipol, people, peapods, peopol, peepol, pîpol; soul, foul, faul, saul, Saul's soul.

"You are just overcomplicating life."

I pause. "I had a book, once."

It was a maths book. Equations. The fact that I was good at maths is beside the point: oh, the elegance of the equation on page 189. Yes, the paper was light and opalescent, you could only add notes with a pencil, possibly using a B, nothing softer. It was also slightly translucent. The ink used for the printing was a dark grey, a cocky grey, a pretended black, but never that dark. Opening that book, at that page, it was like if I saw a slight tinge of warm gold okra embracing every word, letter, symbol, keeping them warm, lifting them up, giving them perspective and depth; holding them there. As when God touched Adam. Not real, of course, since it was only a visual effect; nothing to worry about, the ophthalmologist had said to my mother. But that shade, it was underpinning the meaning of maths, of logic; that is the true and only language. I mean, if we all agree on the same code to be used. The algorithm of life, where all things important are not to be printed but are hidden and can be read between the lines and seen between the signs. The music now is too loud. I really don't like birthday parties.

"The font used was thin and sophisticated, a printed pseudo-calligraphy but still a very beautiful writing; the parenthesis as gentle as waves and warm as hugs; the x's had curls and the y's a long single plat. The construction, of such an equation, was more important than the mental process behind its formulation;" - storeys of skeletal solidity on a papery foundation.

I could probably use maths symbols to write anything and it doesn't have to sound meaningful. What's the symbol for a symbol, I have always wondered? The whole book reminded me of Copenhagen. No one ask me why; I've never been there, either. But I could imagine an old professor who wore not a tie, but tiny frameless glasses, and dressed in comforting shades of beige and greens, explaining the magic of the symbols, the hidden mysteries of a universal language, a code to analyse, befriend, explore and then leave, intact. (He escorts me by my elbow to the table in the corner of the room.) Untouched. Step by step, getting closer to the result, knowing that the closer you get, the sooner it will all end, so you may as well stop searching, stop looking, slowing the whole process down. (He pours wine? I haven't asked for wine.)

"That book, to me, meant hiding away and slowing down. So, now, when I'm writing, I'm trying to reproduce the elegance of that equation on page 189, my personal Rorschach image, slowing my hand when I reach the middle of a page, when I know that I've crossed an unindicated mark, getting closer, and closer, and closer to the end."

And when you get to the end of the page you just stop wherever you are even if the sentence isn't finished. Half way even of a single wo wherever the page imposes its own limit: no more signs no more! Words, and their absence, do not kill imagination. Then my hand gets suddenly dry, the pen feels like powder and there you have it: the absence of masculinity.

"The more I write, the sooner I will have to stop." (I scribble something in the air and then stop).

But instead I am there, adding more words with S's and h's: shell shall she. Sherlock. I like those words, with S's and h's. I really like them. Sh looks like 84. Putting nib to paper is important because I'm alive; my act proves that I breathe, that I was there then. That line I scribbled yesterday shows that I exist. If someone is going to read it, or just look at it, part of me is seen. My encounter with the page is set in time, even if we both have a life beyond that moment. The page has a life on its own, independent: a well-rounded blue morphing into a deep oceanic green. Everchanging albeit unseen, almost cheeky, surprising me every day with a different hue. And what about me? My act of writing is more important than the writing itself. Does a dancer need to know steps and sequence before the music starts? What kind of a sign do I leave behind? I am thinking accessibility, simplification, subtracting synthesis. Reducing to a dot. You can have a whole poem in a single dot. And you will have an infinite international understanding.

"But how do you make money?" he asks while chewing, his mouth full of white bread.

"I have a job.", I mumble.

remission

in the quiet of a wave
the remission of thousand angles
and perception of shadows

a heron

we can now go home.

(1996)

9: *surrounded by*

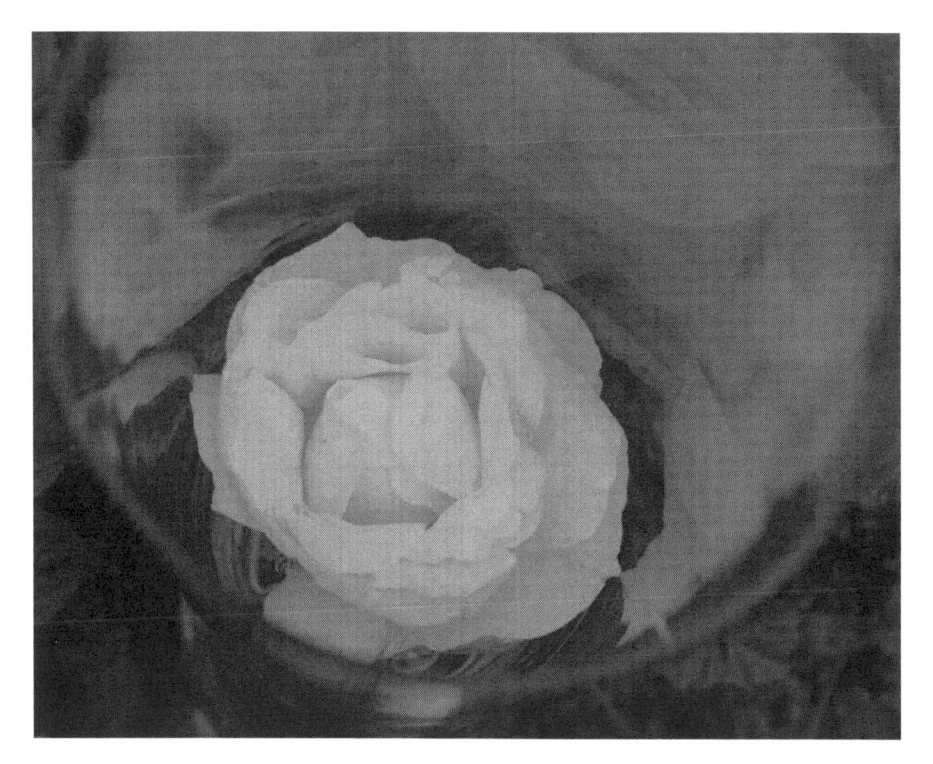

as tempest

as tempest
the other half of my soul
entered in me
only to reveal myself

will I ever love
more closely?

what was his aim
if not to shake me
out of my own torpor?

...

my heart
a chasm
for new light

...

but now
got this
still
the hardest is to let him go.

would be seriously alone.

emptiness.

"fear..."

(260608)

10: liquid sublimation

something cool

> I'd bet you couldn't imagine that I once had a house
> With so many rooms you couldn't count them all
> I'll bet that you couldn't imagine I had fifteen different boys
> Who would beg and beg to take me to the ball
>
> And I know you couldn't picture me
> The time I went to Paris in the fall
> And who would think the man that I loved
> Was quite so handsome, quite so tall
> [SOMETHING COOL : Bill Barnes 1954, as performed by Tierney Sutton 2002]

I don't yet know what it was, but my eyes looked at my hands, and only then did I recognise myself. Time stood still, I stopped breathing, head gently tilted on my right. My eyes, my hands. My eyes, my hands. My hands.

Someone must have called my name because I suddenly woke up from this time-gap and returned to the Body. Where had I been?

I observe my hands as for the first time. My veins as snakes around my tendons and a handful of cappuccino shaded lentigines tossed on my right hand only; the hereditary vertical ridges of my nails. I stretch my hands wide in front of me, as if ready for a *virtuoso* movement on an imaginary piano. The dry hands and thin long fingers of auntie Anna, neither of us a piano player. They say you can love only with your hands; who said that?

Now, it's me, the real me, the thinking me, who is looking at them. But before? I was suspended into a different vacuum, where neither time nor rhythm exist. My Self is questioning whether I was having a stroke. I raise my right arm, I touch my mouth, I hide a pretended smile, just to check my lips. No, everything is fine.

Simply, my soul nudged me into a realisation I can't easily grasp now. I felt I had been catapulted somewhere where everything is clear and then whipped back here crossing corporeal boundaries; not remembering a thing. I can only imagine it was my soul. Or was it the Universe? God? Was I summoned to reality or to the holiness of future emptiness?

Someone is still calling my name, if only for the second time. I turn my face, smile and mumble something like: "sorry, I was away with the fairies…"

I look around and see the people sitting at this table, with me. They are talking, yes, but who are they? I have just woken up.

I do recognize him, and he is checking from the bar if I want to have another drink. I smile, nod, and point at an empty glass in front of me, trying to remember what it was that I drank before. My buds prompt me with a relic of some sweet white wine. I don't remember enjoying it but I still nod, and smile, and pretend that everything is fine; just fine, just perfect.

I sit there, an inane sad smile on my face, a vacuous look, the one I lately surprise myself using when I stare at something into the distance while still wearing my reading glasses and, at the same time, not understanding what is being said. Basically, an idiot. This fleeting thought makes me smile, and I feel entitled to justify my idiocy to myself. Wearing this face, tonight, an idiot becomes the Fool.

Which deceit did I choose for this evening? I gaze briefly, hopefully unobserved, at my legs, covered by a pair of tight black jeans: oh so, this evening it was jeans, a white shirt sufficiently open to reveal cleavage and bra, just enough to scare the possible contenders, or simply future nominees, away. That look that should say: "look at us, we are just so happy"; but as of now it screams: "he has me for as long as he wants, and then when he will leave me, I will disappear engulfed in cellulitis, menopause and forgetfulness". My wittiness and knowledge are a show I seem to put up for his coeval peers: I am shown in public and I wonder why I am not paid a fee for my performance, tonight, like every other Friday night; or maybe his sex earlier is to be considered enough of a payment on account, for me.

"You are so wise; how do you do it?" someone chirps at my left, her flowless mascara winning against my mellow cheeks.

I sense that whatever I cannot give name to, that which was there (here?) before, is now broken, and cannot be mended. The virus has spread and multiplied itself, overhauling; I easily become a puppet in his string-less hands performing in a replica of a 1930 Berlin cabaret, where on this stage, sick and pale, I sing to no audience. Surd in voice and reduction.

A wave of nausea fills me. It's quick, but it leaves behind its marked conduit, for me to fill with… nothing.

I look at my masked face, reflected: it says thirty; or maybe forty, to a stretch. I look at my hands: they don't lie and confirm fifty.

I feel the impulse to answer with words and not just condescending smiles.

"Do you really want to know how I do it - I think - I am 17 years older than him, that is how I do it, bitch". And I stop a smile from turning me into a devilish shark.

I feel rapidly very tired and it is not anxiety. I feel I'm progressively sagging, turning into a wizened week-old retirement balloon. Deposited there. Its purpose already fulfilled and forgotten. My only hope is that I don't turn into ridicule, the poor man's me.

And then I look up again, at my face reflected in this fake aged mirror and I see my mother's empty eyes, recognise the wrong shade of lipstick, a vane hint of sweat under the new perfume. My left hand shakes slightly. He comes back, with two glasses of wine, sits and puts his arm around my shoulders, such a darling. I smell him, I want to remember this moment so close to death.

"How did I end up here, Mother?" I ask the reflection.

She doesn't really reply. But, suddenly, I recognise it for what it is. Desolation. Deep slowly rolling misery. Thick like molasses, it doesn't allow itself to be cried out. I feel like drowning, while still trying to reach the banks which could secure my safeness. A place to rest and breathe. But I can't. He talks and I gasp for air; his thigh touches mine, oh! so not fair, and I drown in my own sporadic wetness; I look at his lips and I let go. The golden thick syrup turns into a black rolling river of regrets and I feel slurped into this swamp. A second wave of nausea and I feel urged to choose between public sadness or solitary death. Or both, lucky me.

Maybe it all started this afternoon, when in the shop I was trying on new jeans, breaking in new shoes, smelling of an incoherent combination of *eau*, and in the mirror I saw these punctured, deflated and humiliated boobs, there, in the cubicle, humbling asking for acknowledgement.

I now converse in Converse while this new sterile me is judiciously discerning the words to use: shall I match the topic or shall I match the show? I am constantly assessing the act, the requests, the performance: not so much that I'm overdoing it, never not enough that I am found disappointing (tz tz...) and hence easily forgettable. Still, what am I doing here? For the second time in a week he did not grasp a reference from a Seinfeld episode. How could he, he was only 10.

At times I am wondering if, between him as a very private fornicator, and him misplacing a subjunctive right after the act, I ever felt the urge, the animalistic impulse, ever, to smother him.

"Look, we are wearing matching shoes and jeans!", I blurted out the other day. "Twins!".

"Well, not really twins, coz you are older than me", he laughed back. We both laughed, open mouthed, one overstressing and the other one underlying the unbelievable fun we were having.

And I recognise now that my puppeteer has never become the puppet. My peers look at me as if asking: "really?" I don't react: brainwashed, unsensitised, lobotomised. I am, in unwilful wonder, drawn into this downward spiral I am only part consciously aware of.

I could break the falling, I could stop. I could leave.

I could ask for help.

I am zeroed.

I see them, the old happy ones all going shopping on Saturday afternoons, carrying meaty Sunday newspapers to National Trust properties for which they have paid the annual membership, filling up flasks and enjoying the squeakiness of leather boots.

He now kisses me on the temple, which is so 'grandmother smelling of lavender and wearing powdery pink cardigans'. Staring into nothing, I am wondering where I have left my hypothetical flask. That connection, that connection of before, that realisation, is right here, right now. I raise my eyes, look in the mirror, and I see me: a mischievous smile I cannot stop, slightly impish; and I feel a bit of a lonely rascal. If I have to do it my way, I need to smile, I need to be me. I will be blunt.

I stand up, adjust my shirt, grab my bag, smile at him. I really don't know how to put it but I am filled with an impetus given by the realisation that the real me doesn't actually give a shit.

"Gotta go".

I turn.

I am out.

I breathe.

in that dream

in that dream
where the fire was winning
defeating itself

ceasing to be
and you were vomiting in my mouth

at waking
my awakening
pregnant at last
frank of freedom
conscious.

(200608)

11: weariness

drafted in pain

I went to his funeral today, mum. And now I'm fucking angry. I tried to remind myself to not look at his kids, but I couldn't. You could see that she had been crying and he tightened his jaw as he walked briskly past me, a perfect haircut and fists in his pockets: such a little hardened man. Oh, mum... she is so young. She was dressed in grey and reminded me of myself at that wedding in the valleys when I was only young and you dressed me up in some candy-pink shirt and itchy tights. How can a funeral remind me of a wedding?
She looked so proud, and so desperate. Barely ten and already so old, carrying the weight of undefinable emotions. No one touched her, held her, helped her, assisted her, exhorted her. Nothing, no one. She was surrounded by withheld breaths. So, she walked. All these adults, mum, all so engrossed in their own pain to forget this little woman with the name of a flower.
Even her mother, shaking hands and proffering smiles.
This is why I am angry, mum. Because at his funeral, today, I heard all the funny tales and the jokes and the stories, and not one, so

absorbed in their pain they were, mentioned where I met him; because he was one of my clients, mum.

And, you see, I get them, mum, when they are already feeling better: their hands don't shake that much, when they walk they don't stumble while laughing, their bodies don't smell, and when they talk they don't slur. What they say makes finally sense, even through their denial. I never see them asleep on the sofa, dribbling in slime, in front of the TV. I never see them chocking on their own food when they remember to eat. I never see them hiding anything, hoarding salvation, lying through their teeth. I never see them when they wet themselves in the middle of the street and the neighbours point, laugh, and then walk away.

When I see them, mum, they don't remind me of you.

But I know that when I walk into the large living-room, I still see him, half asleep, with his big smile. He was always there.

The day he died I went and sat in his spot, closed my eyes, hoping to understand, yearning for a connection, maybe an excuse. Even an accusation. Nothing.

Trying to conquer the unconquerable, this feeling of inability and constantly hitting a dead-end is, at times, unbearable. Mum, it's excruciating, torturing, horrifying. Can you feel my impotence, Mother?

So, now, I'm sitting at my white table, mum, drinking Pinot Noir and I really do hope I get pissed, swallowed by the bottle. I am pouring and pouring red wine because it's the one easier to cry to; and I have that melody on repeat, that sad one, that one that sucks me in and makes me miserable every time. Because too many times I have been that little girl, too many times; and today, at the funeral, I just wanted to take her home with me, mum, because telling her that, in the end, "everything is going to be fine" is not fucking enough. The tales of redemption, and life after death, the battles of George and the Dragon, the meaning of life and the purpose of his death and her tears will not fill that void of having lost her dad. Today should have been a day for snot, hiding and rocking in someone's arm, not for theology and reasoning.
What was she doing there, really?

She will never see her dad again.

This is final. Absolute and ultimate.

That's it.

.

And she had no choice, no vote nor veto.

Tonight, mum, I want to cross that boundary for her; and reach you. And experience what it means to feel such a desperation, hopelessness and desolation and still feel the burden of carrying on with your life; that life, your life; I want to visit that place where living is such an agony that you experience the absurdity of needing to create pain not to feel any pain. You need to create pain to have the illusion of feeling a speckle less pain. Mum help me, because I don't get it: I want to know what it is, mum, because maybe, after tonight, I'll be just good enough that there will be no more little girls at funerals.

[...we went for a pizza, that evening (do you remember?)

after dad's funeral...]

find/ness me

festinating
head inclined
chime in

I.
       (who dances bare feet)
grinning alone
stretch forth arms.

            he.
            (who cannot scream)
will (I) am await/ing
privilege expectant
in inclination I dawdle
            un-unveiled.
to endowment am patient
in acquisition engrossed

ingratiating, irrigate a desert

of my unblushing optimism
               a victim.

to confidence
sentenc/sed breeder

of stones farmerette
           disillusioned

engrossed by admiring
eclat-ness flourish
in what is pure/ly only seed

mongrelling hope
to see what is not.

a hair of grass
won't ever sing

and as oil on *Mario* I slue away

(072008)

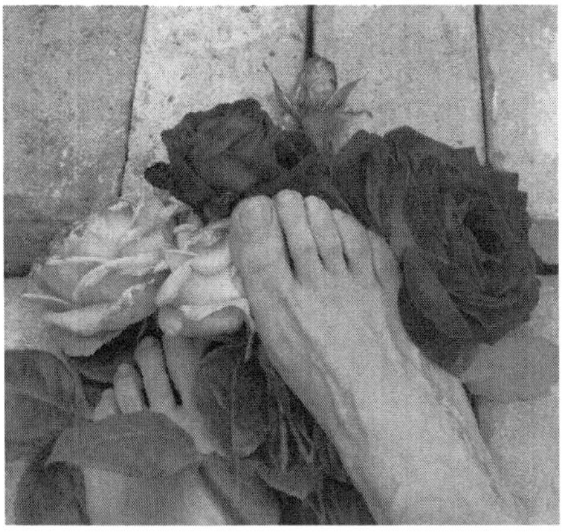

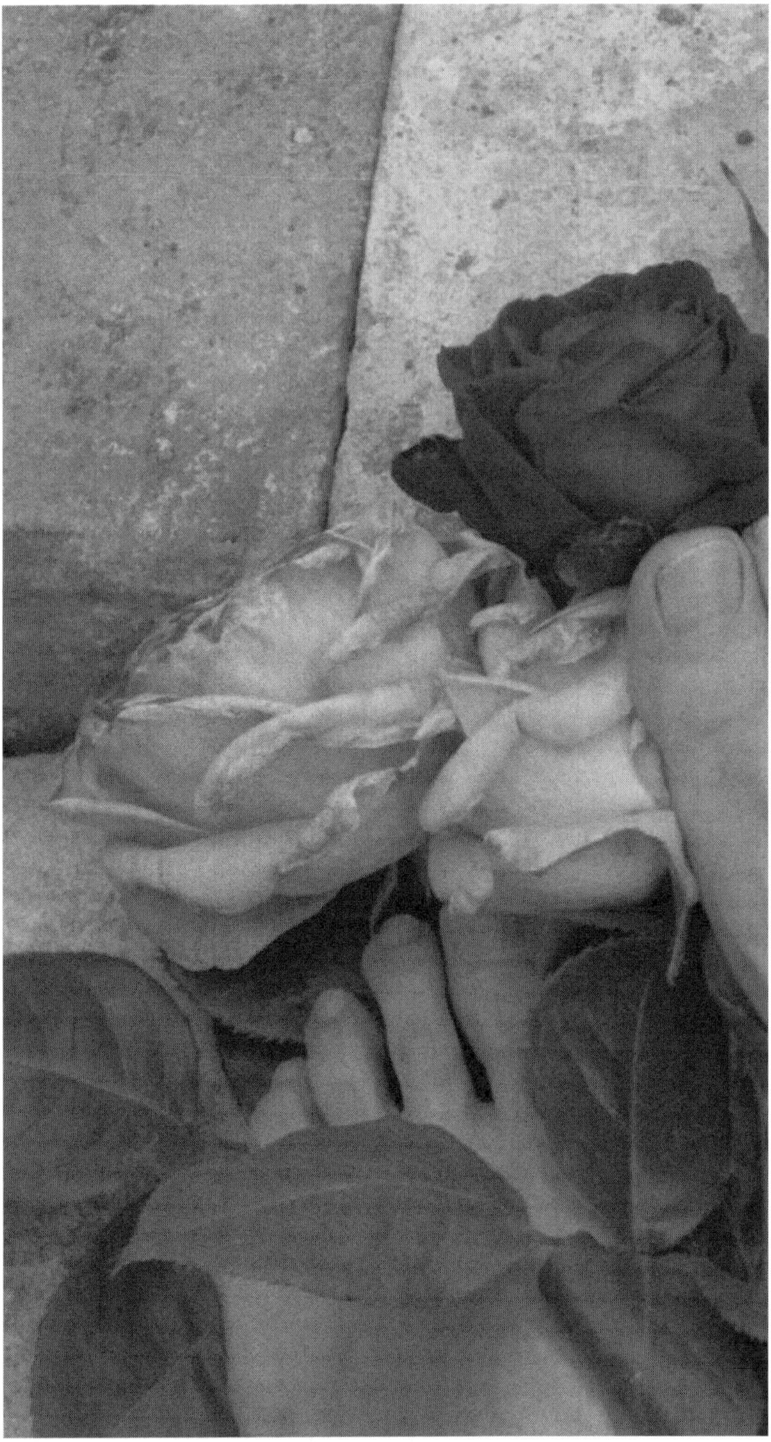

12: immaculate misconception

Printed in Poland
by Amazon Fulfillment
Poland Sp. z o.o., Wrocław